the egg

the pumpkin

Mrs. Snake

the feather

Uncle Rabbit

the eyetooth

Mr. Lion

the pumpkin whistle

Mr. Eagle

With thanks to Dr. Ana Rosa Núñez,
Research Librarian, Otto G. Richter Library, University of Miami,
for sharing her knowledge, her poetry, and her friendship;
to Alma Flor Ada, Lulu Delacre, and Lucía Gonzáles
for reading the manuscript and offering such good advice;
and to Dr. Beatriz Varela
for researching *pitos de calabazas*

V O C A B U L A R Y

Águila (AH-ghee-lah) Eagle

la calabaza (kah-lah-BAH-sah) pumpkin

el colmillo (kohl-MEE-yoh) eyetooth

gracias (GRAH-see-us) thank you

el huevo (WAY-voh) egg

León (lay-OHN) Lion

Papá Dios (pah-pah dee-OHS) Father God

perdón (pear-DOHN) pardon me

el pito (PEE-toh) whistle

la pluma (PLOO-mah) feather

por favor (POOR fah-VOOR) please

señor (sen-YOOR) Mr., sir

señora (sen-YOOR-ah) Mrs., madam

Serpiente (sair-pee-EHN-tay) Snake

tío Conejo (TEE-oh koh-NAY-hoh) Uncle Rabbit

Rabbit Wishes

by

Linda Shute

Lothrop, Lee & Shepard Books
New York

Inquiries should be addressed to Lothrop, Lee & Shepard Books, a division of
William Morrow & Company, Inc., 1350 Avenue of the Americas, New York,
New York 10019. Printed in the United States of America.
First Edition   1 2 3 4 5 6 7 8 9 10
Library of Congress Cataloging in Publication Data
Shute, Linda. Rabbit Wishes: a Cuban folktale / by Linda Shute.
        p.   cm.   Includes bibliographical references. Summary: Presents an
Afro-Cuban folk tale which explains why rabbits have long ears.
ISBN 0-688-13180-8. 1. Rabbit (Legendary character)—Legends. [1. Rabbit
(Legendary character) 2. Rabbits—Folklore. 3. Folklore—Cuba. 4. Blacks—
Folklore.] I. Title. PZ8.1.S5598Rab 1994 398.24'529322—dc20 [E]
93-45895 CIP AC

It was soon after Creation that *tío Conejo* began to complain. *Papá Dios* had made him with silky soft fur, long fuzzy feet, and short shapely ears, but he was not content. He wanted to be bigger.

So he complained to *Papá Dios*. "O Creator of all the animals," said the rabbit, bowing low. "Did you mean to make me so small? I wish I were large like Elephant, or tall like Camel, or at least as big as Goat."

"I made you just the right size," *Papá Dios* replied. "You are comely, clever, and swift. Be satisfied as you are."

But *tío Conejo* didn't know when to hush. "It's no use being handsome or speedy or smart when I'm too small to be noticed!" he whined.

"Enough!" said *Papá Dios*. "I'll think about making you bigger. But first you must bring me three things: a feather from *Águila*, the eagle; an egg from *Serpiente*, the snake; and a tooth from *León*, the lion."

Feather, egg, tooth. *Una pluma, un huevo, un colmillo.* How could *tío Conejo* ever take them from Eagle, Snake, and Lion? Those three hungry hunters would eat him for lunch! All they ever thought about was their next meal.

And that gave *tío Conejo* an idea.

First he made a whistle from the stem of the pumpkin, *la calabaza.* Then he went in search of *señor Águila.*

As soon as he spotted the eagle circling in the sky, *tío Conejo* blew on his whistle: *whee-o, whee-o, whee-o.*

Down swooped *señor Águila*. "What is that rude sound?" he screeched. "Stop it, or I'll eat you at once!"

"Ah, *señor Águila*, I would stop it if I could," said *tío Conejo*. "But *Papá Dios* put a magic hair in my fur that whistles each day for my supper. He must have made a mistake. All it brings are fish and egrets and coots—when I eat only green sprouts and roots."

Fish and egrets and coots! Those were the eagle's favorite foods. If he had that magic hair, he would never have to search for a meal again.

"*Tío Conejo*," said *señor Águila*, "I am sure *Papá Dios* meant that hair for me. Give it to me, and I'll forgive your rudeness."

"*Gracias, señor Águila*," said *tío Conejo*. "Allow me to remove a feather and plant my hair in its place."

That made sense to *señor Águila*. "Certainly," he replied.

So *tío Conejo* plucked a feather from the eagle's wing and pretended to make the trade. "You must sit very quietly until the hair starts to whistle," he warned. Then, while *señor Águila* waited to hear *whee-o, whee-o, whee-o, tío Conejo* sped away with *la pluma*.

Next *tío Conejo* set out to find *señora Serpiente,* the snake. She was dozing in the sun beside her nest. From a safe distance, he blew on his whistle: *whee-o, whee-o, whee-o.*

Señora Serpiente woke with a start. "What's that noise disturbing my sleep?" she hissed. "Stop it, or I'll eat you at once."

"*¡Perdón, señora Serpiente!*" called *tío Conejo.* "It is my magic hair that whistles for my food. *Papá Dios* put it in my fur, but he must have made a mistake, for all it brings me are mice and rats—when I eat only lettuce and radishes."

Now *señora Serpiente*'s favorite foods were mice and rats. She imagined how easy her life would be if they marched right into her mouth.

"*Tío Conejo*," she said, "I'm sure that *Papá Dios* meant that hair for me. Give it to me, and I'll let you pass."

"*Gracias, señora Serpiente*," said *tío Conejo*, "but it won't whistle unless I plant it in your scales."

That made sense to *señora Serpiente*. "Of course," she replied.

"You must stretch out straight and lie very still," said *tío Conejo*. "If you move a muscle, my hair will not take root." Then he hopped onto her back and dug his claw deep into her skin as he snatched an egg from her nest.

"Ouch!" yelled *señora Serpiente*, but she did not move. She was still waiting for the whistling hair to take root when the rabbit got home with *el huevo*.

Finally *tío Conejo* stood trembling outside the den of *señor León*. Would his trick work one more time? He took a deep breath and blew on *el pito de calabaza*.

"How dare you insult me with your *whee-o, whee-o, whee-o!*" roared *señor León*. "One so disrespectful should be eaten!"

"*Por favor, señor León*," *tío Conejo* begged, "the sound came from my magic hair. *Papá Dios* put it in my fur to whistle for my food, but he must have made a mistake. All it brings me are goats and cows—when I eat only oats and carrots."

"Goats and cows are my favorite foods," growled *señor León*. "Clearly *Papá Dios* meant that hair for me. Hand it over, and I'll ignore your insult."

"With pleasure, *señor León*," said *tío Conejo*, "but it won't whistle unless I plant it beneath your chin."

That made sense to *señor León*. "Do it immediately," he ordered, and lifted up his head.

Tío Conejo reached for a rock while he scratched the lion's chin. "Now, hold your mouth open so the food can run in," he said. Then, WHACK! he hit the lion's eyetooth. "Open wider!" he exclaimed. "The first goat bumped his horns and ran away!"

Greedy *señor León* stretched his mouth as wide as he could, and the rabbit yanked out the tooth. Then, while the lion waited for the second goat, *tío Conejo* raced away with *el colmillo*.

The next morning *tío Conejo* placed *la pluma*, *el huevo*, and *el colmillo* before the Creator.

"See, little rabbit?" said *Papá Dios*. "You were clever enough to take these prizes from creatures much larger than yourself. You don't need to be any bigger."

"But you promised!" cried *tío Conejo*.

"I promised I would THINK about it," said *Papá Dios*, "and I have thought—about how much more trouble you'd be if you were any larger. You are perfect just as you are. Go, and be content."

But *tío Conejo* still did not know when to hush. "You promised," he whined as he turned to leave.

Of course, *Papá Dios* heard him. Instantly *tío Conejo* felt his ears stretch. Suddenly they were as long as his long fuzzy feet!

"You have ruined my short shapely ears!" *tío Conejo* wailed.

"Now you are bigger," said *Papá Dios*. "I have granted your wish. Do you have another?"

"But my ears . . . ," *tío Conejo* began. Then he shut his mouth. Perhaps it would be wiser to learn to love long ears.

SOURCES FOR THIS STORY

Elephants and camels never lived in Cuba as they do in *Rabbit Wishes*, but they lived in the memories of the African slaves who were brought to Cuba during Spanish colonial times. These people from the Congo River basin and West Africa passed on African traditions and beliefs to their descendants just as European settlers perpetuated their Spanish heritage and Native Cubans preserved theirs. Over the centuries, these separate traditions have often merged, but there remains a distinctive African-Cuban culture with its own unique music, art, religion, and folktales.

Sociologist and folklorist Fernando Ortiz (1881–1969) pioneered transcribing African-Cuban oral traditions at the beginning of this century and founded the Archives of Cuban Folklore in 1924. During the 1950s, Lydia Cabrera (1899–1991), an artist and leading writer on Cuban folklore, also recorded numerous African-Cuban tales of gods, spirits, and anthropomorphic animals including *tío Conejo*. The collections *Leyendas Cubanas*, by Salvadore Bueno (b. 1917), and *Cuentos y Leyendas Negras de Cuba*, by Ramón Guirao (1908–1949), contain many of these wonderful folktales—including the explanation of how the rabbit got his long ears that inspired *Rabbit Wishes*.

Pumpkin Whistles

While researching this book, I discovered people from Cuba, Spain, and even Romania who used to make pumpkin whistles like *tío Conejo*'s as children. Now adults, they recall carving *pitos de calabazas* from the stems and sometimes part of the shell of pumpkins or squashes. The whistle emitted a high, shrill note when blown—the sound described in this retelling as *whee-o, whee-o, whee-o.*

In Cuba, whistling is a sign of disapproval. *Tío Conejo* is being extremely rude when he whistles at *señor Águila, señora Serpiente,* and *señor León.*

Tío Conejo

Stories about *tío Conejo* are told throughout Latin America. In Nicaraguan and Guatemalan variants of this tale, the trickster rabbit collects the skins of monkeys, alligators, and tigers in order to claim his reward. Our Cuban *conejo* is less bloodthirsty—closer in spirit to the African-American character Brer Rabbit. But while Brer Rabbit always emerges victorious from his exploits, none of *tío Conejo*'s clever schemes works out quite as he expects.

Linda Shute
Miami, 1995

señora Serpiente

el huevo

la calabaza

tío Conejo

la pluma

el colmillo

señor Águila

el pito

de calabaza

señor León